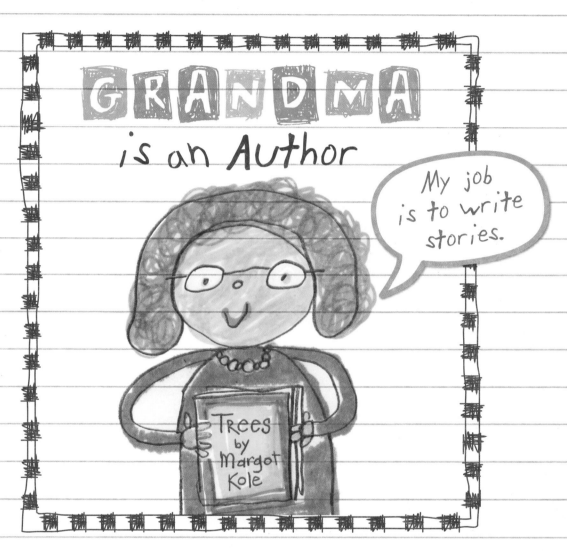

GRANDMA
is an Author

My job is to write stories.

Trees by Margot Kole

Melissa Conroy ★ drawings by Elliot Kreloff

🍎 BLUE APPLE BOOKS

Meet Margot, my grandma.

This is me, Rusty.

Margot writes books for grown-ups.
They are called novels.
Margot makes up the whole
story, so her books are "fiction."

I like to draw pictures while
my Grandma writes.

I wonder how
Margot writes
so many words.

Her glasses look like two squashed circles.

Sometimes we write stories together.
Today we are writing about sand castles.

Yesterday we
wrote about
a praying mantis
named Troy.

We also wrote about an apple tree that grows green apples. I called them "Granny Margots!"

It was my idea to make the tree a home for a family of purple caterpillars.

On Grandparents Day at school,
guess who I brought? Margot!

Ms. Francesca asked everyone
to introduce their grandparents.
Here they all are:

Ms. Francesca

Margot

Room 202

Milo's
Grandma

Ruby's Grandma

Jonathan's
Granddad

Milo told us that his grandma is an artist. One time, she asked all of her friends to send her a piece of toast. She arranged the toast and glued it onto paper until it looked like a flower. Then she put it into a beautiful frame.

Toasted Petals

This is my grandma. Her name is Naomi.

Jonathan's granddad is a high school history teacher. He likes to take Jonathan on walks through the park. Here is Jonathan sitting in a tree.

Ruby's grandma is a nurse. They have a secret handshake. She teaches Ruby card tricks. I'm going to ask Ruby to show me a trick.

When it was my turn, I said,
"My grandma, Margot, writes books.
She doesn't go to an office to work.
She spends the whole morning typing
lots of words in
her writing room.
She has good
stories to tell."

This is a book that Margot wrote.

BEACH WALK
by MARGOT KOLE

Margot stood up and spoke to the class.
"I love to write. When I pick up a book,
I enjoy the feel of it in my hands.
I like the sound of pages turning.
Even the smell of books makes me happy."

Kevin raised his hand.

Margot answered Kevin's question.
"I decide what to write. Usually,
the words come easily, but sometimes
they don't. I have what is known as
'writer's block.' That means you're
stuck and you don't know what to write."

Jonathan asked, Can you take medicine for writer's block?

Clara asked,

How do you make writer's block go away?

"There's no medicine for writer's block.
It doesn't hurt, but I have to be patient.
The more I worry, the worse it gets."

"So when that happens, I take a break and
do something else, like walk on the beach."

"If that doesn't help
and I am stuck,
I play the flute . . .

or bake a cake."

"After a while, the writer's block goes away."

I thought about writer's block
on the way home from school.

I imagined heavy blocks,
like bricks, squashing
Margot's words.

I wondered,
"Is writer's block
a ghost that makes
the words in your head
misty and cloudy?"

At home, I got my sketchbook.
I drew really fast. When looked down,
I saw a big monster in the scribbles.

I looked at the monster for a while.
Then I had an idea—
an idea to help Margot
when she is blocked.

I went to the kitchen, and I found:

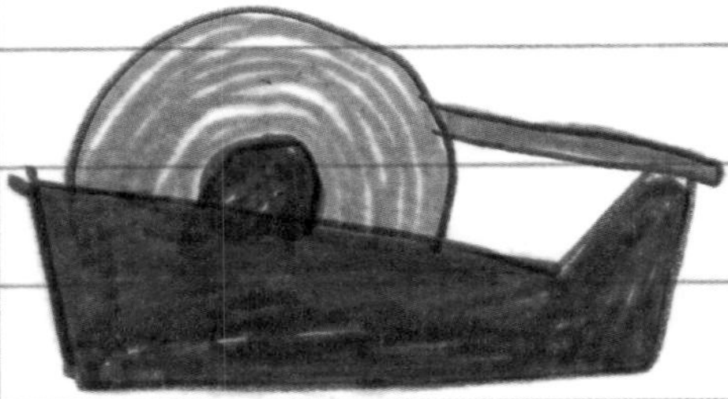

tape

scissors

glue

crayons

pipe cleaners

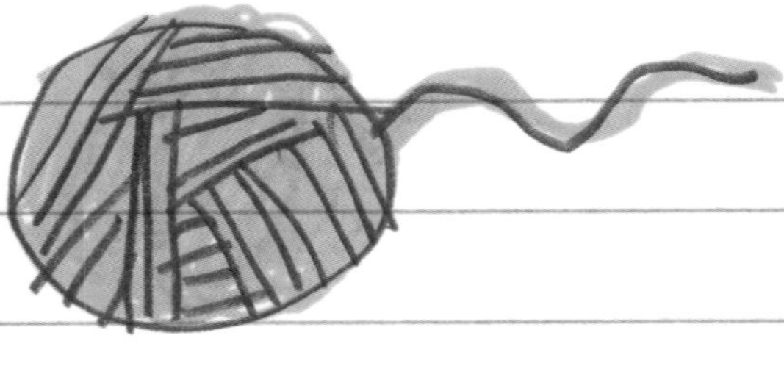

string

colored paper

The recycling bin had:

cupcake holders   small cardboard boxes

paper towel tubes

big cardboard box

buttons   yogurt cups

old scrub brush

I took everything to my room.

I taped.

I glued.

I colored.

I built.

DONE!

I stepped back to take a look.

This monster was not right. I did not think
it would help Margot with writer's block.

I felt like getting mad, but instead,
I lifted up my monster and looked
him in the eye.

This monster
couldn't scare
anyone or anything!

"Much better," I said.
"I am going to call you Gus."

"I am going
to put you
to work."

I took Gus to Margot's writing room.
The door was closed. I stood at
the door for a minute, then I knocked
as loud as I could.

Margot opened the door and asked,

I said, "Gus is here to help you.
His teeth are big and strong,
and he has lots of ideas in his head."

"If writer's block comes around,
  Gus will scare it away or eat it for lunch!
  Then he will help you find the words."

Margot smiled. She put Gus on a shelf where she could see him from her writing chair.

Then we sat down to write together.

I am lucky to have a grandma who's an author and who helps me write stories.

For my boys, Wester and J.
—M.C.

Text copyright © 2011 by Melissa Conroy
Illustrations copyright © 2011 by Elliot Kreloff
All rights reserved / CIP data is available.
Published in the United States 2011 by
🍎 Blue Apple Books,
515 Valley Street, Maplewood, NJ 07040
www.blueapplebooks.com
First Edition   9/11 Printed in Shenzhen, China
ISBN: 978-1-60905-039-9

2   4   6   8   10   9   7   5   3   1